What Grandmas Can't Do

To all grandmas and
little monsters everywhere,
and to my grandmother,
Blanche Wilton—D. W.

To Juney and Millie,
Grandmas true.—D. C.

❤ ALADDIN PAPERBACKS
An imprint of Simon & Schuster Children's Publishing Division
1230 Avenue of the Americas, New York, NY 10020
Text copyright © 2005 by Douglas Wood
Illustrations copyright © 2005 by Doug Cushman

Designed by Lucy Ruth Cummins
The text of this book was set in 20-point Garamond Bold.
The illustrations for this book were rendered in pen-and-ink and watercolor.
Manufactured in China
First Aladdin Paperbacks edition March 2008
1 2 3 4 5 6 7 8 9 10

The Library of Congress has cataloged the hardcover edition as follows:
What Grandmas can't do / Douglas Wood ; illustrated by Doug Cushman. —1st ed.
p. cm.
Summary: Lists all the things a grandmother cannot do,
such as baking your favorite cookies by herself,
or opening her purse without finding gum or candy.
[1. Grandmothers—Fiction.]
I. Title: What Grandmas cannot do. II. Cushman, Doug, ill. III. Title.
PZ7.W8473Whi 2005
[E]—dc22
2003027432
ISBN-13 978-0-689-84647-2 (hc.)
ISBN-10: 0-689-84647-9 (hc.)
ISBN-13: 978-1-4169-5483-5 (pbk.)
ISBN-10: 1-4169-5483-X (pbk.)

ALSO AVAILABLE

What Grandmas Can't Do

by Douglas Wood

pictures by Doug Cushman

Aladdin Paperbacks

New York   London   Toronto   Sydney

There are lots of things regular people can do but grandmas can't.

Grandmas can't bake your
favorite cookies by themselves.

Or serve tea.

Or look at picture albums.

They love to tell stories,
but they need a really good listener.

Grandmas can't remember everything.
But they *can* remember when there wasn't any
television or peanut butter yet.
And when your parents were babies!

Grandmas can't be named Heather or Jennifer or Melissa.

Only Grandmother or Grandma. Or Great.

Grandmas can't reach up and down as easily as they used to.

They like having some help.

They can't play Chutes and Ladders or Chinese checkers without laughing a lot.

And sometimes they can't laugh without tears coming out of their eyes.

Grandmas can't open their purse without finding gum or candy.

Or lipstick.

Grandmas can't buy everything in the store.

But they give it a good try!

They can't walk through the yard without spotting a four-leaf clover.

Or a lucky penny.

Grandmas may not know how to use computers,
or video games, or the newest whatchamacallit.

But they're ready to learn.

Grandmas *can* clean the house by themselves.

But they'd rather not.

Same with laundry.

And dishes.

Grandmas can't stand dirty ears.

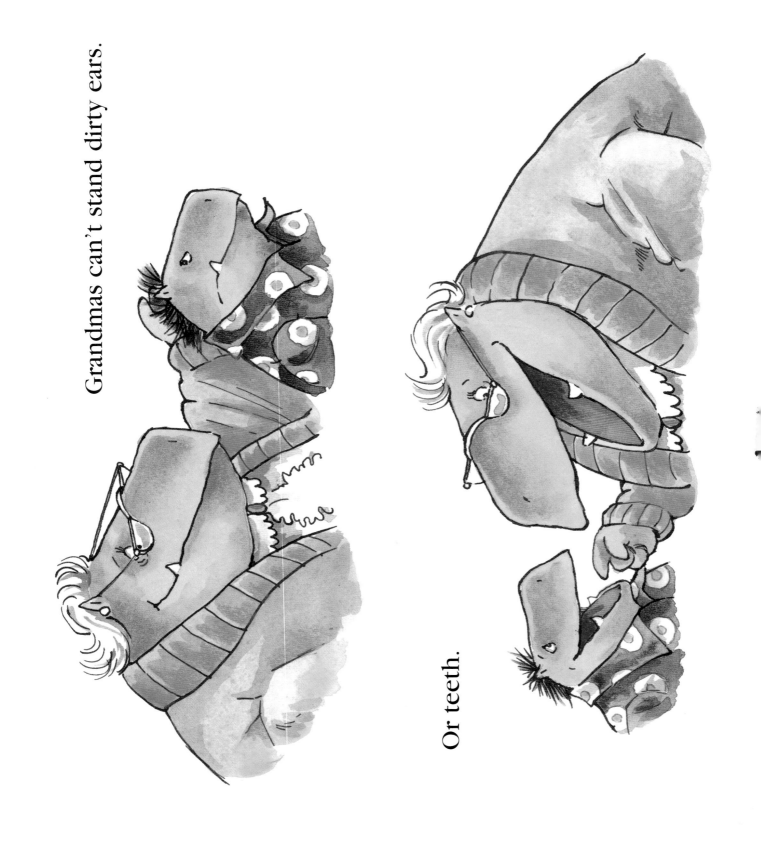

Or teeth.

They can never get
too many hugs.

Grandmas can't let you go to bed without reading you a story—or six.

And getting a kiss.

There are lots of things grandmas can't do.
But they do one thing that nobody else can.

And that's be your
very own Grandma.